W9-BZA-617
ella
AND Olivia

For Camille—YP
For my mum and dad—Mal and Judy—DM

Scholastic Australia
345 Pacific Highway Lindfield NSW 2070
An imprint of Scholastic Australia Pty Limited
PO Box 579 Gosford NSW 2250
ABN 11 000 614 577
www.scholastic.com.au

Part of the Scholastic Group
Sydney • Auckland • New York • Toronto • London • Mexico City
• New Delhi • Hong Kong • Buenos Aires • Puerto Rico

Published by Scholastic Australia in 2012.

Text by Yvette Poshoglian.
Cover design, illustrations and inside illustrations by Danielle McDonald.

National Library of Australia Cataloguing-in-Publication entry

Author: Poshoglian, Yvette.
Title: Ella and Olivia and the cupcake catastrophe / written by Yvette Poshoglian and illustrated by Danielle McDonald.
ISBN: 9781742833545 (pbk.)
Series: Ella and Olivia ; 1.
Other Authors/Contributors: McDonald, Danielle.

Dewey Number: A823.4

Typeset in Buccardi

Printed by McPherson's Printing Group, Maryborough, VIC.

Scholastic Australia's policy, in association with McPherson's Printing Group, is to use papers that are renewable and made efficiently from wood grown in responsibly managed forests, so as to minimise its environmental footprint.

10 15 16 17 18 / 1

By

Yvette Poshoglian

Illustrated by

Danielle McDonald

A Scholastic Australia Book

Chapter One

Ella and Olivia are sisters. Ella is seven years old. Olivia is five-and-a-half years old. They live with their mum and dad and little brother Max.

Ella is busy baking. She is wearing an apron and holding a wooden spoon. A packet of flour is open.

There are sprinkles of flour everywhere. Ella doesn't mind getting a little bit messy when she cooks.

Olivia is helping Ella in the kitchen. She helps her big sister with everything! Together they are looking for two mixing bowls. Ella is going to make one mixture. Olivia is going to make another.

There is a recipe book propped up on the counter. It is called *Cupcakes for Princesses*. Mum bought it for them. She thought it would be perfect for *her* little princesses!

Ella and Olivia aren't *real* princesses. But they *are* going to make cupcakes.

Ella has a long ponytail and green eyes. Olivia wears pigtails and has freckles. Her hair is a little bit lighter than Ella's for now. But Olivia hopes it will be the *exact* same shade one day.

The girls' little brother, Max, doesn't have a lot of hair yet.

But when he does, it will probably be the same colour too.

One day, Olivia wants to be just like her big sister. Ella is good at netball and likes to draw. Olivia loves dressing up and pretending to be a fairy princess.

Ella and Olivia both **love** to cook!

Ella and Olivia are very good at helping Mum in the kitchen. Max is also helping. He is sitting on the floor of the kitchen, playing with a wooden spoon and a saucepan. Bang, crash! Max likes making noise.

The girls are excited. They are going to make cupcakes for Dad. Dad's birthday party is this afternoon. Mum bought a LOT of candles for the birthday cake.

All the family will be there. Their cousins Charlie and Josh are coming. Uncle Stu and their favourite Aunty Laura are bringing a big chocolate cake.

Nanna and Grandad will arrive in their trusty old kombi van.

'What colour icing should we put on the cupcakes?' asks Ella.

Bang, **crash**, Max answers.

'I like pink,' says Olivia. 'What about you?'

'Ummm,' Ella needs time to think. 'Dad doesn't like pink very much,' Ella says. Then she has a brainwave!

'What about the colours of his favourite footy team?' Ella says.
'Good idea,' says Olivia.

The girls are getting the ingredients ready. Baking is fun, but first you have to make sure you have all the right things to put in the mixture.
'Have we got everything we need?' Ella asks.

Olivia inspects the counter. There is flour, milk, butter and eggs.

'Let's start cooking!' says Olivia.

Chapter Two

The girls are going to make two kinds of cupcakes–orange and brown. Those are the colours of their dad's favourite footy team, the Tigers.

'I love cooking,' Ella says. Ella's favourite things to make include toast and cereal.

'I love cooking too,' says Olivia. Sometimes Olivia helps Mum mash the potatoes in the saucepan. 'One day I want to be a good cook like Mum,' Ella says.

MASH

MASH

‘What about me?’ Dad grumbles. He has crept into the kitchen! ‘I can cook, too,’ he says. Dad is good at cooking pancakes, schnitzel and eggs. Sometimes Max tries to help him.

But right now Dad should *not* be in here. The cupcakes are a surprise! ‘DAD!’ cries Ella. ‘We told you not to come in!’ Ella can be very bossy.

'Out you go,' Mum says.
'OK, OK!' Dad says,
backing out of the kitchen.

Mum is reading another recipe, so together the girls start with their own. They carefully measure the flour and the milk. 'Where's the sugar?' Ella asks Olivia.

'I'll get it!' Olivia says. She hops down from the bench. The kitchen pantry is bulging with all sorts of things.

'Which one is the sugar?' Olivia asks.

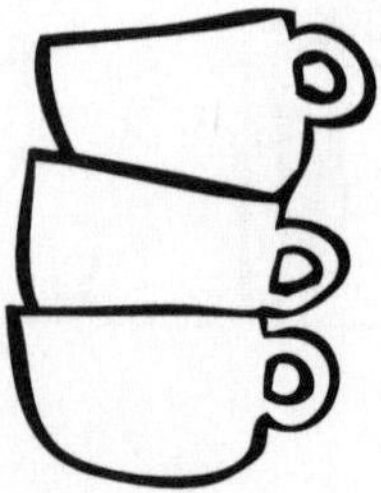

'It starts with an 'S',' Ella replies. It's handy to have a kitchen helper like Olivia! Olivia sees the packet that starts with an 'S'. She can tell from the squiggly lines. It's on a high shelf. It has white paper and pink letters. Olivia reaches up on tippy-toes.

'Got it!' she cries.

The girls measure out the final ingredients and put everything together. They each have their own mixing bowls.

The mixtures get nice and thick.

'No glugs and no lumps,' says Ella. That is the secret to good cupcake batter. It has to be smooth.

'No lumps and no glugs,' repeats Olivia. 'Is that what it says in the cookbook?'

Ella nods. Mum comes over to inspect their work.

'Well done, girls!' she says.

Ella is very excited about the cupcakes. She and Olivia are making them all by themselves—just like big girls! Ella thinks Dad will be very happy.

Mum puts her pretty oven mitts on and checks the temperature of the oven. 'Nearly hot enough,' she tells the girls. 'The next thing you will have to do is put the cupcake mixture into the patty papers,' she says.

Cupcakes are cooked in patty papers, which are placed on a patty pan for baking in the oven.

They have enough room to make twenty-four cupcakes.

'I will make twelve orange cupcakes,' says Ella.
'I will make twelve brown cupcakes,' says Olivia.

They must put one neat spoonful of mixture in each patty paper. Mum helps with the first few.
'Just like this,' Mum says.
She puts a perfect scoop of batter into the patty paper.
'I hope mine can be as neat as Mum's,' says Ella.

Olivia hopes so too. It takes a few tries. Soon they get the hang of it.

The girls neatly scrape the sides of their bowls. Then they are finished.

Ella and Olivia can't wait for the cupcakes to be ready!

Chapter Three

Mum puts the patty pan into the oven. The timer has been set. Now they have to wait for the cupcake to bake.

Tick-tock.
Tick-tock.

The minutes tick by. Ella looks at her watch.

'How much longer?' asks Ella.

'About twenty minutes,' says Mum. 'A watched pot never boils,' she says. Instead, Ella and Olivia help Mum clean up. They clear the counter. They wipe down the mess.

Now they have to make the icing for the cupcakes. Together, they get the next round of ingredients ready for Mum. There is icing sugar, cream cheese, butter and hundreds and thousands.

'Ding-a-ling!' the oven cries. Mum checks the oven. The cupcakes have risen! They puff up over the patty papers.

'Good girls, Ella and Olivia,' Mum says. 'It looks like you have perfect cupcakes!'

The girls can't wait to see what they look like. Mum takes them out of the oven. She rests them on a rack on the counter. They smell so good. Ella wants to eat one straightaway.

'Don't touch them yet!' Mum warns. 'You might burn your fingers,' she says.

'They're not for you,' Olivia says. 'They are for Dad,' she reminds Ella.

The cupcakes look lovely and golden on top. They smell yummy.

'Now we are going to make the icing,' says Mum. Ella fetches another wooden spoon from the drawer for her. Olivia holds up *Cupcakes for Princesses* for Mum. Mum puts on her reading glasses.

'A *bit* of cream cheese . . .' says Mum. Ella hands her the cream cheese. It has gone super soft from sitting on the bench, but that's OK.

'A *lot* of icing sugar,' Mum says. Olivia hands her the packet of icing sugar. 'And some butter!'

Mum adds the ingredients to the bowl. She uses the electric mixer.

Whirrrrrrrr!

Ella and Olivia watch. Soon the lumpy, bumpy mixture turns smooth. Mum stops to have a look.

The mixture is a creamy yellow. She takes half of the mixture out and puts it into another bowl.

'One mixture needs to be orange,' says Mum. 'And the other one will be brown.'

Ella is being very careful. She squeezes two drops of orange food dye into one mixture. Then she squeezes two drops of brown food dye into the other.

'Good girl, Ella,' says Mum.
Olivia stirs the mixtures.
One mixture turns orange.
The other turns brown.
'Well done, Olivia,' says
Ella. Little sisters can be
very helpful sometimes!

The guests are nearly here.
The girls put the icing on
the cupcakes and sprinkle
hundreds and thousands
over the top. The cupcakes
look amazing!

'You'd better get ready for the party now, girls!' says Mum.

Ella goes to her bedroom. She knows exactly what she is going to wear. Mum has laid out her favourite lilac dress with white spots.

Ella finds her good shoes in the cupboard. They are shiny patent leather. They have buckles and a very small heel.

Ella goes into the kitchen and does a twirl. Mum is braiding Olivia's hair into a plait. Olivia has a new dress and her favourite shoes on. 'We're ready!' the girls shout together.

Mum claps. 'So are the cupcakes!' she says.

Chapter Four

The girls are nervous and excited. The cupcakes look so pretty. They want Dad to be happy on his birthday. But will the cupcakes taste as good as they look?

Both girls have signed the birthday card. Ella drew it especially for Dad. She loves to draw. Olivia added

a flower and Max drew
a special line in orange
crayon.

'Have you got Dad's
present ready?' Mum asks.
'Yes!' says Ella. She has the
gift in her hands. It is a
joke book. Dad needs some
new jokes. Ella read it first
just in case. She read some
out loud to Olivia too. It is
very funny.

Dad and Max put balloons on the front gate. There is even a sign that says PARTY! The balloons are orange and brown—a perfect match for the cupcakes.

Ella feels very pretty in her dress.

'Hurry up, everyone!' cries Olivia. They can't wait for their cousins to arrive.

The cupcakes look delicious. But before the girls can do a taste test, the doorbell rings.

Ding-dong!

The guests start to arrive! Nanna and Grandad are at the front door.

Grandad is wearing a tropical shirt. Nanna has bright pink earrings on.

'Hello, you two!' They gather the girls into a big hug. Nanna smells like roses. Grandad doesn't.
'We have a secret!' says Ella.
'What is it?' whispers Nanna. She is very good at keeping secrets.
'We made something for Dad,' whispers Olivia.

The girls take Nanna and Grandad by the hand to the kitchen.

'Ooooh!' says Nanna.

'CUPCAKES?' says Grandad, a bit too loudly.

'SHHHHHHHHHHHH!' whisper both girls. 'It's a secret!'

Ding-dong goes the doorbell again. More visitors have arrived!

Olivia runs to open the front door.
'Josh and Charlie!' Ella cries. 'Charlie and Josh!' Olivia cries. Their twin cousins are dressed in matching shirts and shorts. They have sandy-brown hair and freckles. Freckles run in the family.

Soon, everyone is in the kitchen. There are lots of sparkling, fizzy drinks and fruit juices. There are chips and lollies, and a big plate of strawberries and mango. Aunty Laura has hidden the birthday cake in the fridge.

'Guess what we made? Guess! Guess!' Olivia asks Josh. Josh shrugs. He has no idea.

'Ummmm . . .' he says.
'We made delicious CUPCAKES!' Ella says, showing her cousins the tray from behind her back.
The boys lick their lips.
'YUM!' says Josh.
'Did you make them, Ella?' asks Charlie.
Ella nods. 'Olivia helped me. So did Mum,' she says. 'I hope you like them!'

Chapter Five

It's time for the party to start. The presents have to be opened! Dad is very excited. He loves birthdays. He tears open wrapping paper and ribbons.

He snorts when he reads his cards.

Dad gets some new socks and a t-shirt. He even tries on his new swimming goggles.

He wears them to unwrap Ella and Olivia's present. Dad carefully pulls at the wrapping paper. Ella isn't sure Dad can see through the goggles.
'*100 Jokes for Dad!*' Dad holds up the present.

Everyone claps. Max burps loudly. He is excited, too.

Dad opens up the book. He snorts again.

'What time is it when an elephant sits on your fence?' Dad asks.

Ella knows the answer. 'Ummm . . .' says Grandad. 'Ahhh . . .' says Uncle Stu. Olivia remembers the answer too. Ella read it to her. 'It's time to get a new fence!' she cries. Then everyone laughs. Dad has a big smile on his face.

Soon it is time to have the birthday cake. And the cupcakes, too!

'We must put the candles on the cake,' Mum says to the girls. It takes a long time! Mum and Aunty Laura light the candles.

Ella and Olivia carry their trays of cupcakes out to the table.

'Happy birthday to you, happy birthday to you,' everyone starts to sing. Dad goes red. He takes a deep breath and blows out the candles. Everyone claps. Mum cuts up the cake.

‘Look at you, clever cooks,’ says Dad. His princesses have made cupcakes. ‘Are the cupcakes for me?’ he asks.

He takes a brown cupcake and bites into it. Ella waits. Does it taste good?

Dad's face is a puzzle. He chews and chews and chews. *This is not a good sign,* thinks Ella. Oh dear. Dad looks confused.

'I think you should try one,' he whispers to Ella. Ella picks an orange one. She bites into it. The icing is sweet. But the cupcake is . . . *salty.* She can barely swallow it. **YUCK!**

'Uh-oh,' says Mum. She takes a bite.

'I think you might have used salt instead of sugar in the batter.'

Oh no! Ella feels terrible. This is a cupcake

CATASTROPHE!

Now no-one can eat the pretty cupcakes.

'I can't believe we made salty cupcakes!' Ella says. 'Olivia and I spent so much time baking. We did everything perfectly.'

Then Ella realises. Olivia is still learning to spell. And Ella didn't check the ingredients. That's how the salt was put in instead of the sugar.

'We're so sorry, Dad!' Ella and Olivia say.

'Don't worry,' Dad says. 'You girls are the best. I will never forget that you made me something so special!'

Ella and Olivia soon forget about the cupcakes. There are more presents to unwrap and games to play.

Happy birthday, Dad!

THESE BOOKS ALSO AVAILABLE:

To find out more go to:
EllaandOlivia.com.au
where you can play games and do more fun stuff!